# DON'T FORGET THE OATMEAL!

## A WORD BOOK

### By B. G. Ford
### Illustrated by Tom Cooke

## A SESAME STREET/READER'S DIGEST KIDS BOOK

Published by Reader's Digest Young Families, Inc.,
in cooperation with Children's Television Workshop

apples
oranges
milk
eggs
paper napkins
soap
peas
peanut
butter
hamburger
meat
pickles
bread

**refrigerator**

One morning Ernie and Bert were getting ready to go to the supermarket. Ernie was checking the shopping list to make sure he had written down everything they needed.

"Let's see," he said. "Apples, oranges, milk, eggs, paper napkins, soap, peas, peanut butter, hamburger meat, pickles, and bread. Is that all, Bert?"

"You forgot to write down oatmeal, Ernie," said Bert. "You know I like to have a bowl of delicious, nutritious oatmeal every morning."

"Don't worry, Bert, we won't forget it," said Ernie as he picked up his piggy bank and hurried out the door.

At the fruit stand outside the supermarket, Bert weighed the apples on a scale while Ernie got the oranges.

"Why do you have that string tied around your finger, Bert?" asked Ernie.

"To help me remember the oatmeal," said Bert.

Just then along came Cookie Monster.

"Cookies on sale today," he said, pointing to a large sign. "Cookie will buy enough cookies to last all year!"

ONE DAY ONLY!
Cookies on Sale
49¢ a bag or box

grapes

watermelon

scale

blueberries

strawberries

pears

plums

lemons

cherries

apples

plastic bags

peaches

grapefruit

oranges

Inside the market, Ernie and Bert began to gather the rest of the things on their list.

"We need milk and eggs from the dairy counter," said Ernie.

"What about the oatmeal, Ernie?" asked Bert.

"Later, Bert, later," said Ernie as he hurried to get the milk and eggs.

cream

eggs

milk

Ernie came running back to the shopping cart. "Look what I found, Bert, old buddy! I got some terrific Cheesie Pleasie, and here's some delicious Ice Cream Supreme!"

"But we just need milk and eggs!" said Bert, looking at the shopping list. "You'll have to put those other things back."

At the end of the dairy aisle, Cookie Monster was putting some cartons of milk in his cart. "Mmmm!" he said. "Milk delicious with cookies!"

Bert pushed the cart into the next aisle to look for napkins and soap. Suddenly Ernie came running up behind him with his arms full.

paper cups

sandwich bags

straws

bath soap

dish soap

trash bags

foil

paper plates

plastic wrap

laundry soap

"Wait just a minute, Ernie!" said Bert. "We don't need paper plates and cups today! We don't need sandwich bags and straws! We need only napkins and soap...and *oatmeal*! You'll just have to put those other things back!"

celery

tomatoes

lettuce

carrots

potatoes

onions

While Ernie put back the things they didn't need,
Bert went along to the next aisle to get the peas and
peanut butter.

"Why don't you buy some vegetables, Cookie?" asked
Bert as he weighed the peas. "Vegetables are good for
you."

Cookie ate a handful of peas. "Mmmm! Peas not bad,"
he said.

"Good," said Bert. "Don't forget to pay for them."

Ernie stopped at the meat counter.

"One pound of hamburger meat, please," he said to the butcher.

"Here you are!" said the butcher.

salami

ham

chicken

hamburger

bologna

sausages

liverwurst

bacon

lamb chops

steak

hot dogs

After getting pickles at the delicatessen, Bert checked the shopping list. Then he noticed the string tied around his finger.

"I mustn't forget the oatmeal," he said.

"Did you say OATMEAL?" asked Cookie Monster, running down the aisle. "Cookie *loves* oatmeal cookies! Where do they hide cookies in this supermarket, anyway?"

"Why don't you try the next aisle?" asked Bert.

puffed corn

corn flakes

rice puffs

shredded wheat

pies

Cookie Monster looked into the next aisle....
"COOKIES!!" he shouted.

cookies

cake mix

rolls

pancake mix

bread

crackers

"Yummy!" cried Cookie Monster, running toward the shelves and grabbing a bag of cookies.
    "Oatmeal cookies!

"And peanut butter cookies! Cowabunga!

"Coconut macaroons! Delicious!

"Marshmallow cookies!
Oh, gimme lots of these!

"And Mint Chipparoos!
"And chocolate fudge creams!"

By the time Ernie and Bert reached the bakery aisle to pick up bread, they found Cookie Monster on the floor, surrounded by bags and boxes of cookies.

"We'd better help Cookie clean up this mess," said Ernie.

"He doesn't need all these cookies," said Bert, picking up a box.

Ernie and Bert put things back where they belonged and reminded Cookie Monster to pay for the cookies he had broken and eaten.

cash register

magazines

Finally Ernie and Bert pushed their cart up to the checkout counter to pay for their groceries.

"Gee, Ernie, I thought we'd never finish our shopping."

"It's a good thing I brought my piggy bank along, Bert," said Ernie. "We have just enough money for everything."

cashier

paper bag

checkout counter

books

Ernie and Bert hurried along Sesame Street, carrying their bags of groceries.

Cookie Monster headed straight home for his afternoon snack of cookies and milk.

Back home in their kitchen, Ernie and Bert took the groceries out of the bags. Bert put the jars in the cabinets and Ernie put the milk and eggs in the refrigerator.

Bert read the shopping list again: "Apples, oranges, milk, eggs, paper napkins, soap, peas, peanut butter, hamburger meat, pickles, and bread...."

"OH, NO!" Bert said with a groan, collapsing into a chair.

"What's the matter, Bert, old buddy?" asked Ernie.

Bert held up the finger that still had a string tied around it.

"We forgot the OATMEAL!"